Grand Canyon Discovery

An Activity Book For Kids!

FUN AND FACTS FOR THE YOUNG READER!

American Educational Press

A Division of Double B Publications

Grand Canyon Discovery explores the wonders of the Grand Canyon from the geological formations to the history, hiking, and adventure that abound.

Grand Canyon Discovery combines fascinating facts with creative activities. The young reader can participate in the reading experience and create an adventure in learning!

Written by Bobbi Salts
Illustrated by Steve Parker

Double B Publications
4113 N. Longview
Phoenix, AZ 85014 USA
(602) 274-6821

ISBN #0-929526-03-1

Printed in the United States of America

Copyright © 1989 by Double B Publications-All Rights Reserved.

Reproduction of this book by the classroom teacher for use in the classroom is permissible.

Reproduction of these materials for an entire school system is strictly prohibited.

TABLE OF CONTENTS

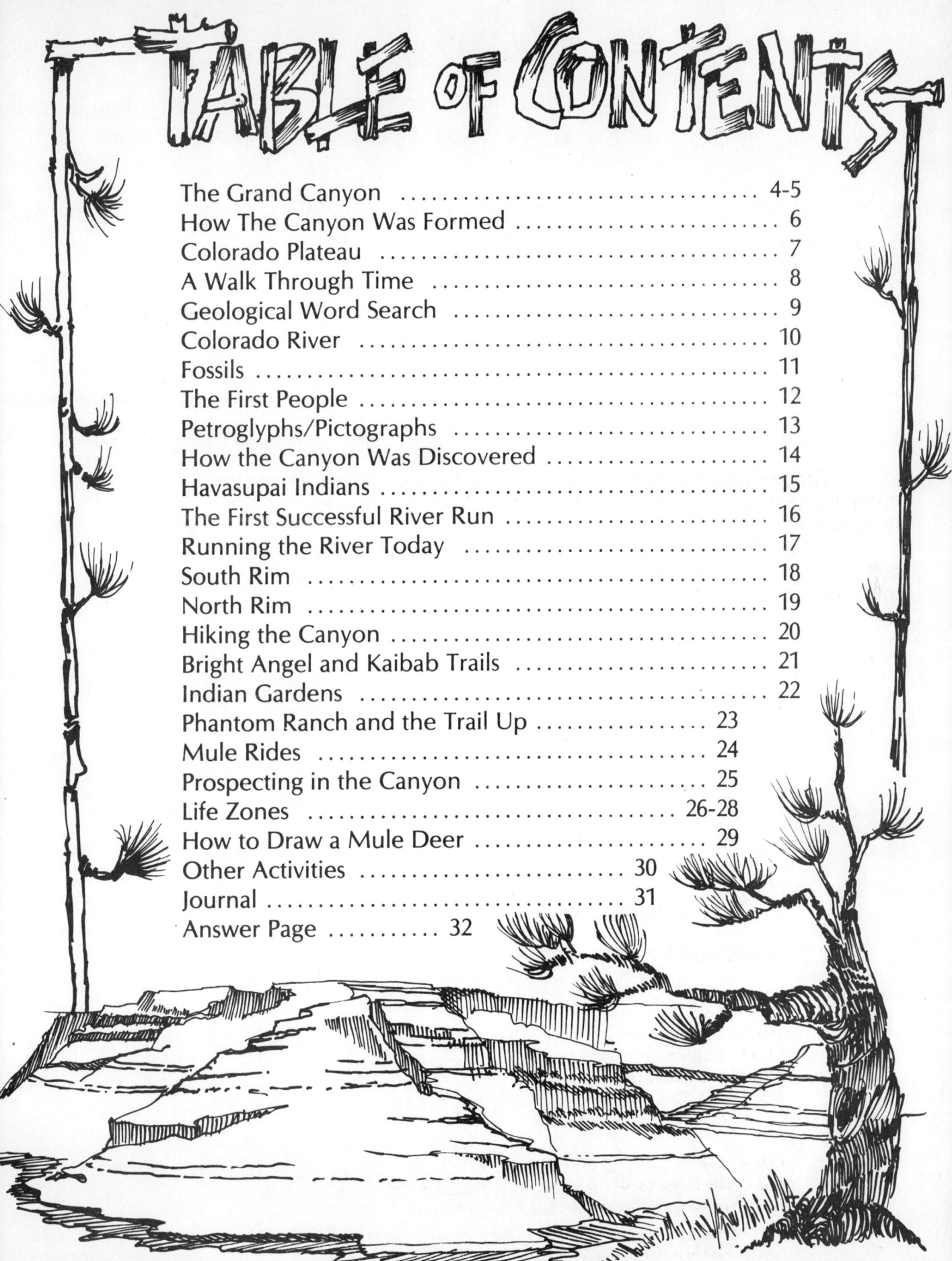

The Grand Canyon	4-5
How The Canyon Was Formed	6
Colorado Plateau	7
A Walk Through Time	8
Geological Word Search	9
Colorado River	10
Fossils	11
The First People	12
Petroglyphs/Pictographs	13
How the Canyon Was Discovered	14
Havasupai Indians	15
The First Successful River Run	16
Running the River Today	17
South Rim	18
North Rim	19
Hiking the Canyon	20
Bright Angel and Kaibab Trails	21
Indian Gardens	22
Phantom Ranch and the Trail Up	23
Mule Rides	24
Prospecting in the Canyon	25
Life Zones	26-28
How to Draw a Mule Deer	29
Other Activities	30
Journal	31
Answer Page	32

The Grand Canyon

Becky and Andy are visiting the Grand Canyon for the first time. Join them in their adventure. Come see why people say a visit to the canyon is like taking "a walk through time."

There is no place like the Grand Canyon in all the world.

You can see many layers of the earth, some of which are two billion years old! The Grand Canyon is 227 miles long and a mile deep. It's about 18 miles straight across from the North Rim to the South Rim. No wonder this is one of the "Seven Natural Wonders of the World"!

1. NEVADA
2. ARIZONA
3. LAKE MEAD
4. COLORADO RIVER
5. SOUTH RIM
6. NORTH RIM
7. UTAH
8. LAKE POWELL

Find your state and color it.

Draw a line from your state to the Grand Canyon

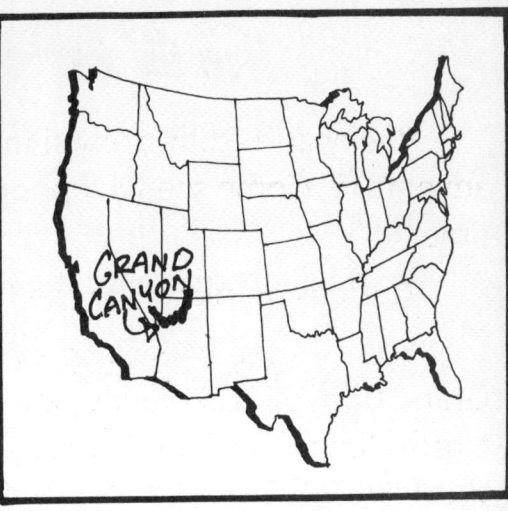

GRAND CANYON

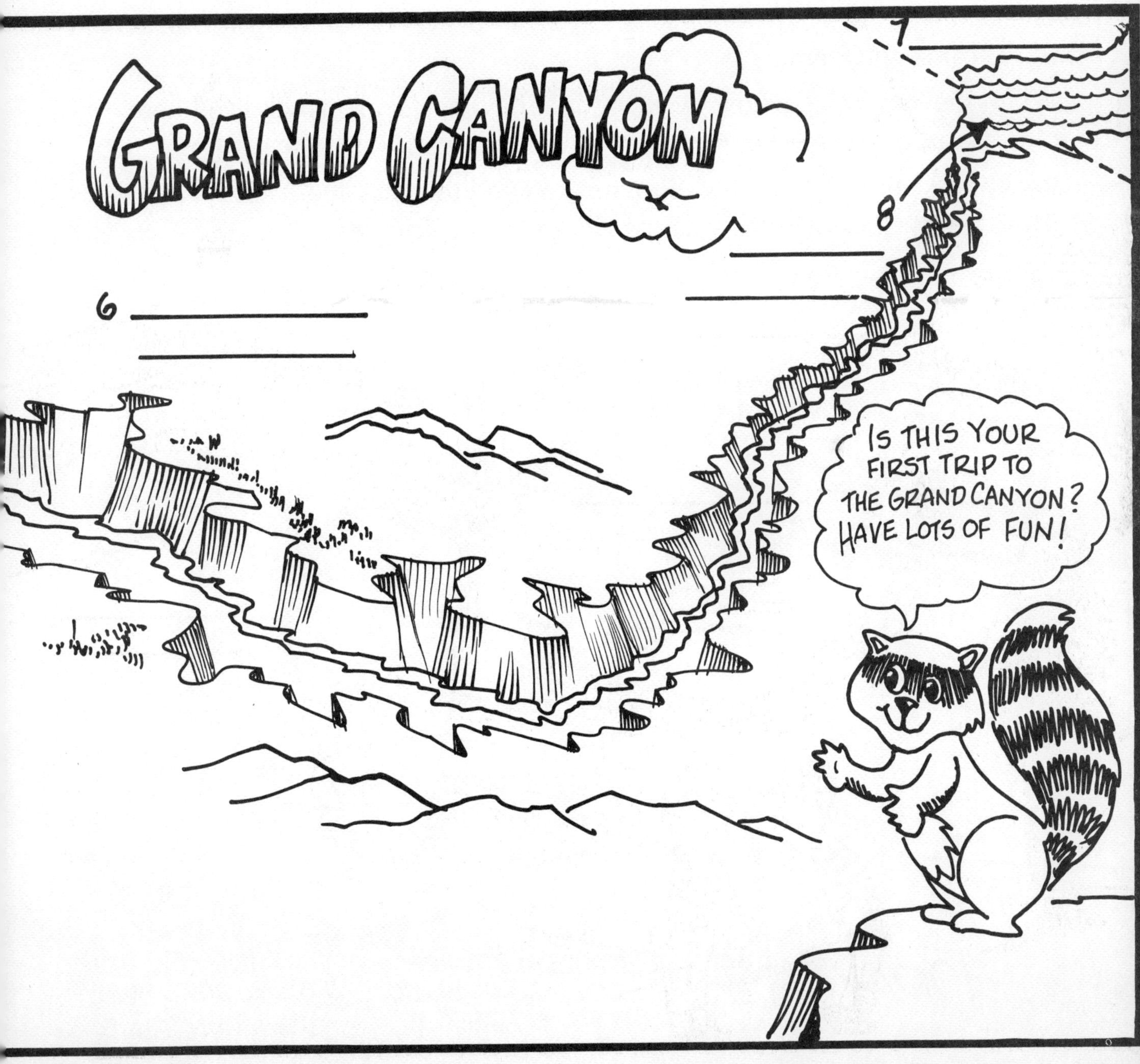
GRAND CANYON
6
7
8
IS THIS YOUR FIRST TRIP TO THE GRAND CANYON? HAVE LOTS OF FUN!

How the Canyon Was Formed

Becky and Andy had a hard time imagining how the earth looked billions of years ago. There were volcanoes, tall mountains, swamps and seas. Each helped form the canyon.

Two billion years ago the land was covered by a shallow sea. Volcanoes erupted. The deposits formed the oldest rock in the canyon, Vishnu Schist.

The land pushed upward forming mountains. They were worn down by erosion. Again a shallow sea covered the land. Mud and sand collected on the bottom of the sea. Once again mountains formed. Erosion again wore away the mountains. Layer upon layer of the canyon was formed as the seas came and went.

When the land was covered by water, marine plants and animals lived here. Their fossils can still be seen in some layers of the canyon.

Becky and Andy learned that dinosaurs roamed the area about 150 million years ago. Then the canyon included swamps, deserts and volcanoes.

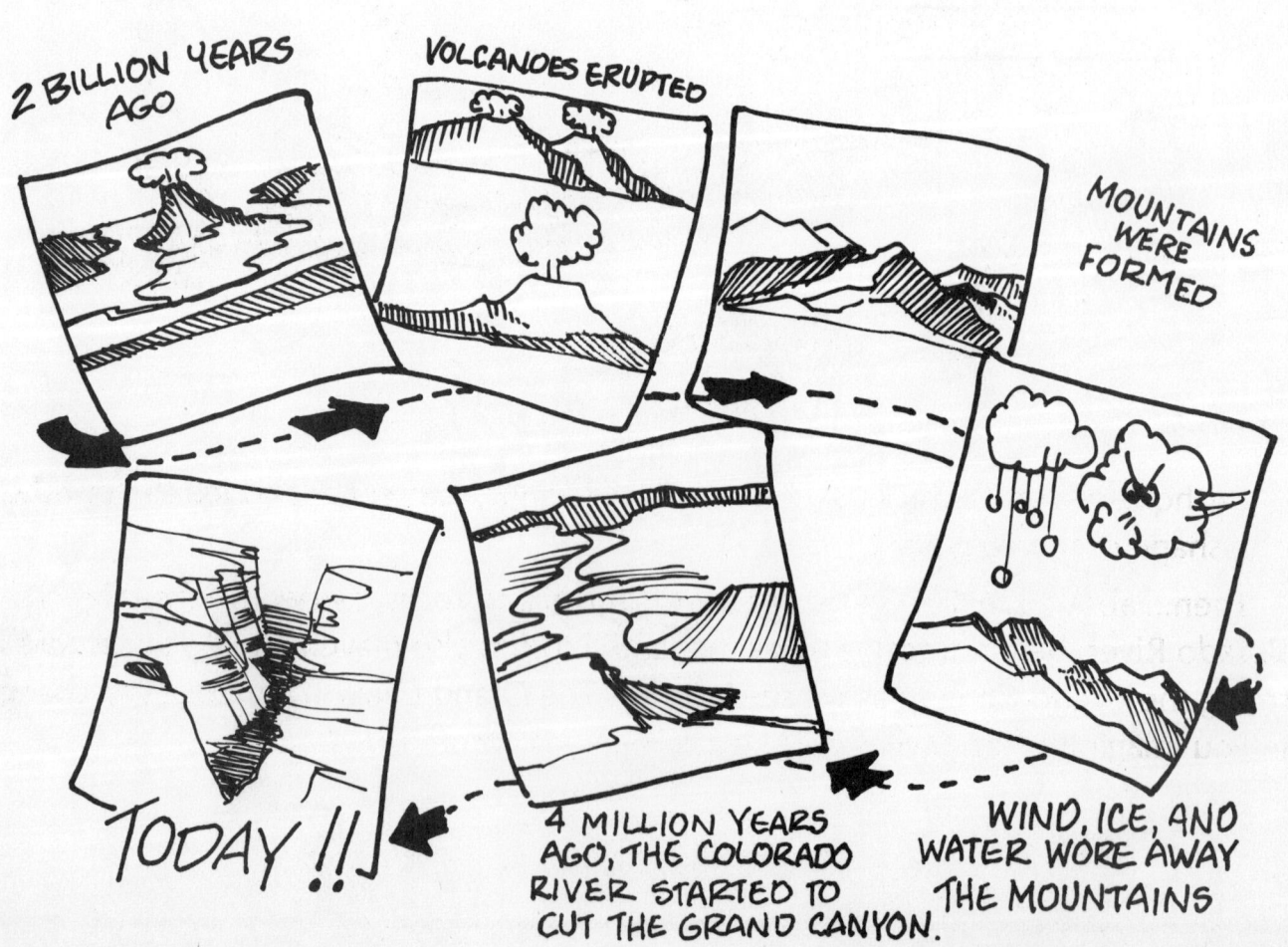

Colorado Plateau

There was a great land uplift for 130,000 square miles. It is called the Colorado Plateau. The Grand Canyon was part of the great uplift.

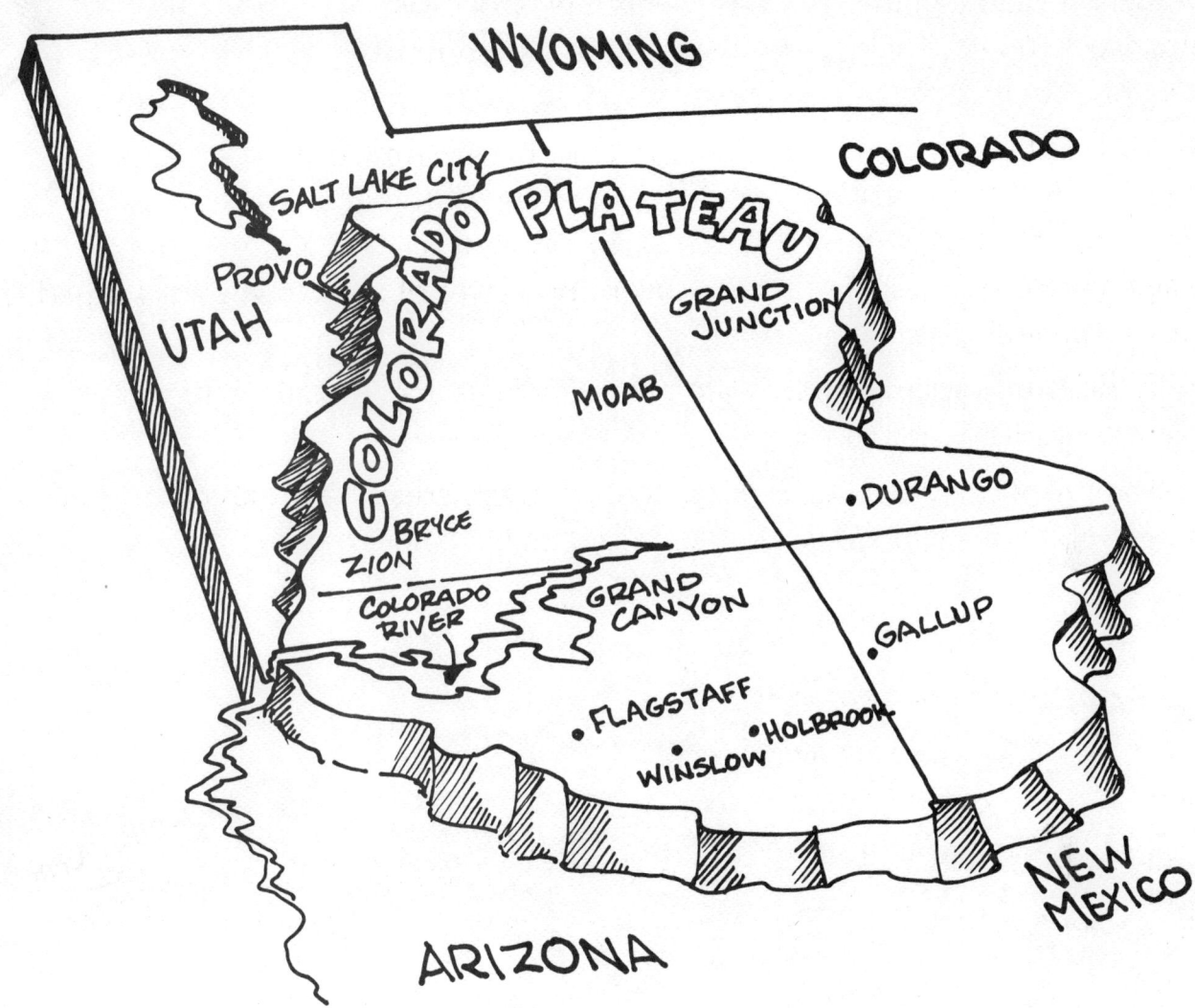

Earthquakes, great cracks, volcanoes, harsh winds, rain, snow and ice all contributed to the shape of the canyon.

Then... about 6 million years ago, sand, gravel and rocks, carried by the mighty Colorado River, began to carve away the land. Erosion also played an important role in forming the Grand Canyon as we see it today. The Grand Canyon continues to change. Can you imagine what it will look like a million years from now?

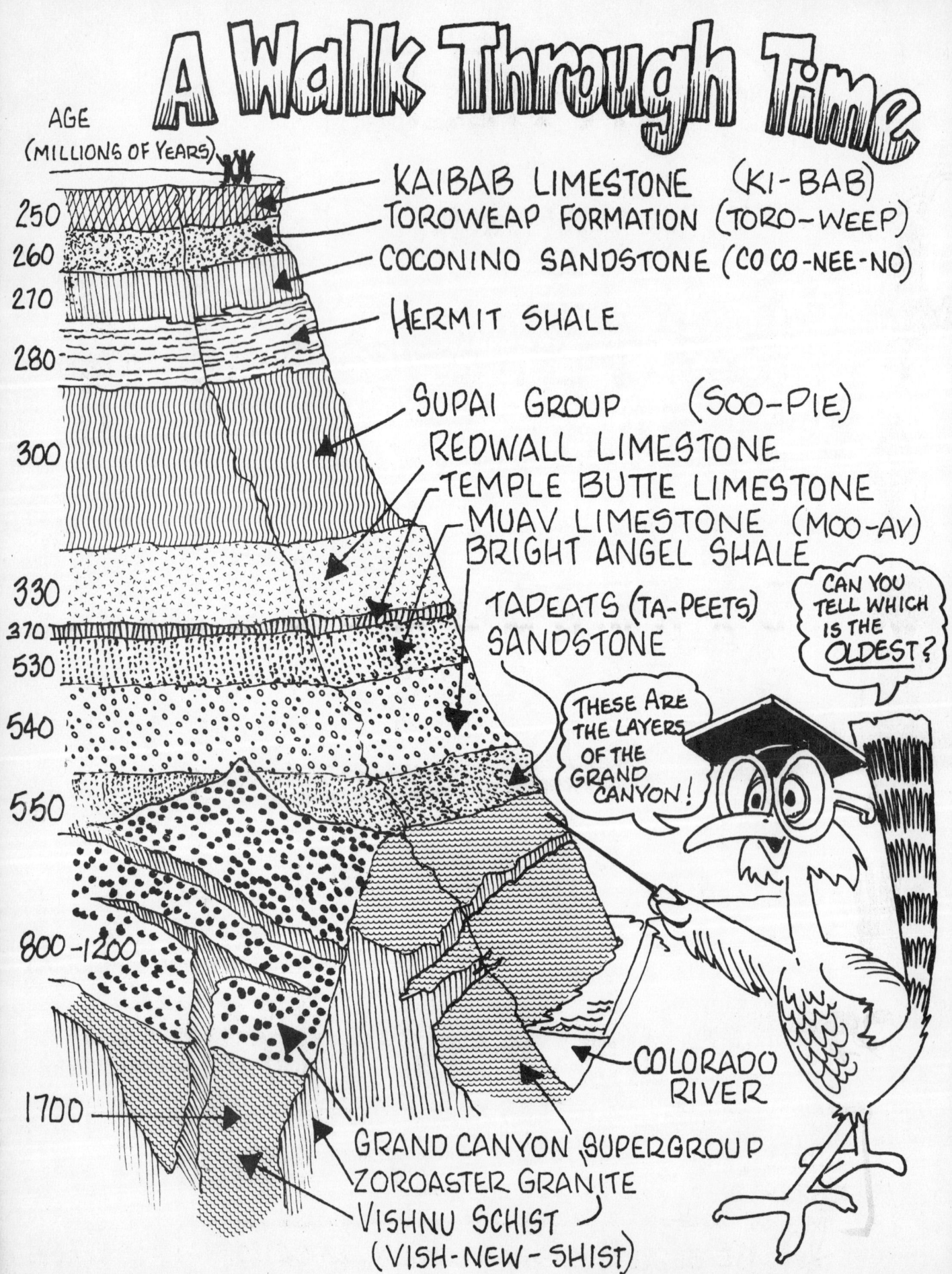

Geological Word Search

```
C T D N B D S J B X P H
D O I T E I Q Y Q Z Q Q
X R C I K K I V N X P I
D O Z O Q Z L X M V Z G
H W T G N L Z O A P B B
F E D A A I L O U D U V
K A R W P M N N E Y V F
G P D E K E H O Q Y W H
R E N I A S A E E R R L
R Y C F I T U T R F Q N
M U A V B O T P S M V E
O N S F A N X O A K I Q
C N J F B E V U D I W T
```

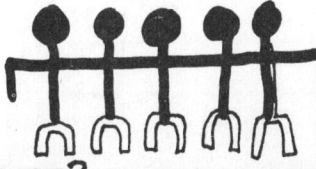

CAN YOU FIND THESE WORDS?

LIMESTONE • COCONINO • TOROWEAP • HERMIT
TAPEATS • REDWALL • VISHNU • KAIBAB • SUPAI
MUAV

✴✴ BE SURE TO CHECK VERTICAL & HORIZONTAL & DIAGONAL

Colorado River

The Colorado river system is over 1400 miles long. It begins at the western edge of the Rocky Mountain National Park and flows into the Gulf of California. There are several branches of the mighty Colorado River.

Today, the river is much slower and more predictable than it was when John Wesley Powell first explored it in 1869. The river's speed is now controlled at Glen Canyon Dam. The dam provides electrical power to surrounding communities. As power is needed, water is released from the dam.

The mighty Colorado River has some of the most dangerous rapids in the country!

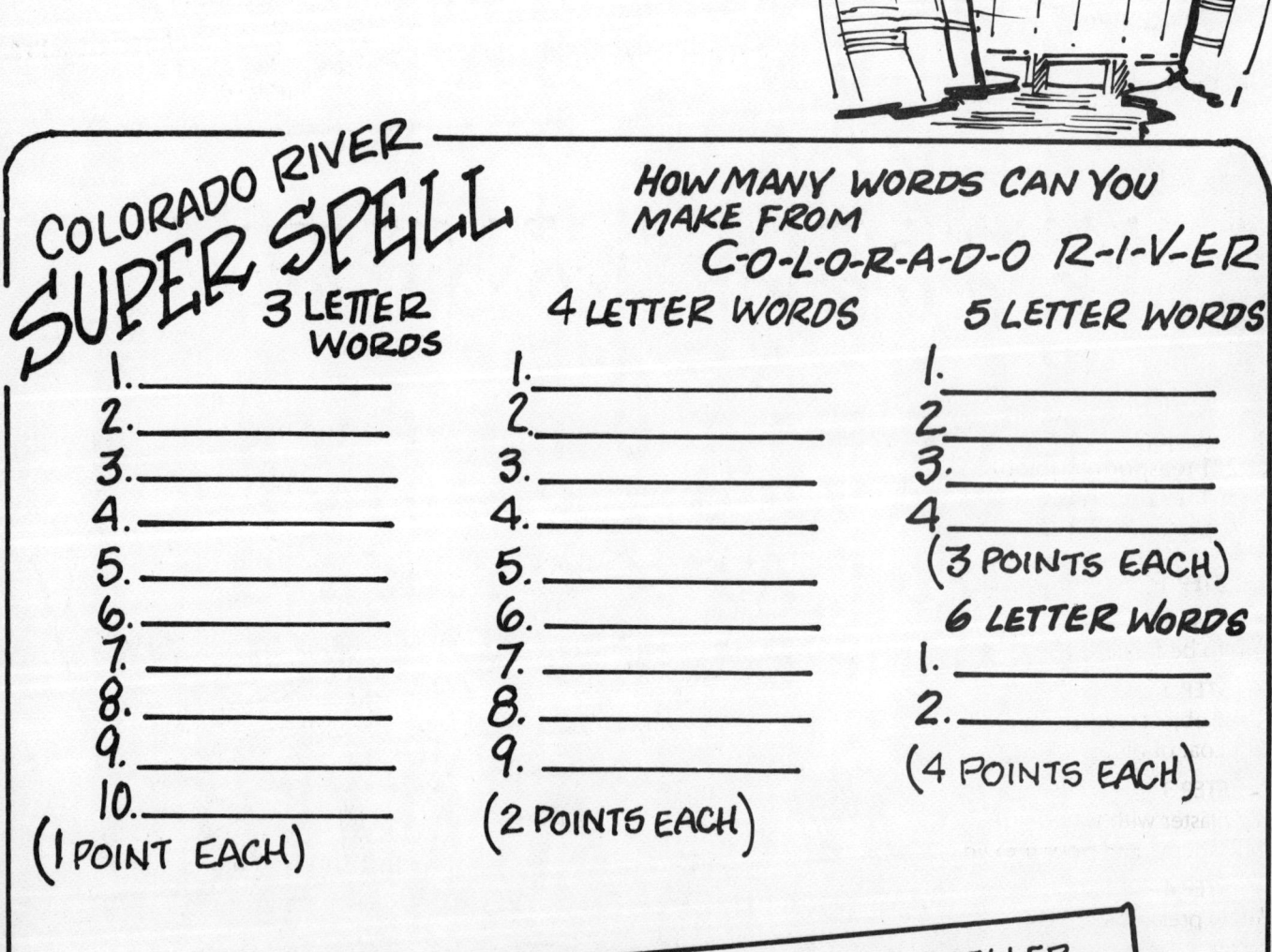

COLORADO RIVER SUPER SPELL

How many words can you make from C-O-L-O-R-A-D-O R-I-V-E-R

3 LETTER WORDS
1. ___
2. ___
3. ___
4. ___
5. ___
6. ___
7. ___
8. ___
9. ___
10. ___
(1 POINT EACH)

4 LETTER WORDS
1. ___
2. ___
3. ___
4. ___
5. ___
6. ___
7. ___
8. ___
9. ___
(2 POINTS EACH)

5 LETTER WORDS
1. ___
2. ___
3. ___
4. ___
(3 POINTS EACH)

6 LETTER WORDS
1. ___
2. ___
(4 POINTS EACH)

YOUR SCORE
3-10 POINTS – CHAMP SPELLER
11-20 POINTS – SUPER SPELLER
21 OR MORE – GENIUS

Fossils

Animals, plants and even footprints from ancient times have been found hardened in stone in the canyon. These remains are called fossils.

Ancient shelled animals called brachiopods have been found at the Grand Canyon. Corals, sponges, snails, trilobites and clams have also been found. These fossils are over 250 million years old.

What kind of fossil would you like to find?

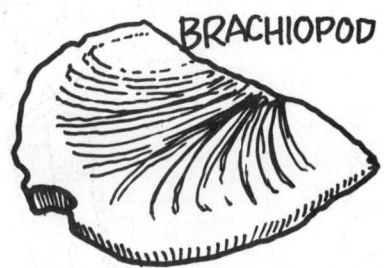
BRACHIOPOD

DINOSAUR TRACK

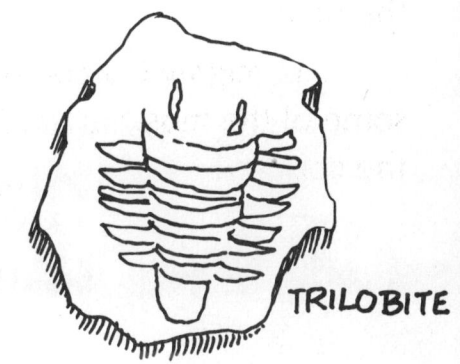
TRILOBITE

MAKE YOUR OWN FOSSIL!

Here's what you'll need . . .
1. fossil object
   (object can be a leaf, toy, coin, etc.)
2. 1 teaspoon cooking oil
3. 1/2 cup casting plaster
4. plastic coffee can lid

STEP 1
Select your toy or item to be fossilized

STEP 2
Cover object with a light coat of oil.

STEP 3
Mix plaster with water until 'soupy' and pour into lid.

STEP 4
Lightly press object into plaster

STEP 5
When plaster is dry, remove object to see your fossil!

The First People

People have lived in the Grand Canyon for thousands of years. More than 2,000 sites have been discovered. These people left behind items that help us learn about their lives.

Split-twig figurines were found in hard-to-reach caves. They are made from willow or cottonwood twigs, split lengthwise, then wrapped into deer and sheep-like shapes. Scientists believe these figurines are 4,000 years old. Pottery, tools and weapons were also found.

Andy and Becky learned that the ancient Indians probably lived, farmed and hunted on the rim in the summer. During the winter, they would move to the inner canyon for a long, mild growing season.

CIRCLE THE TWO PAIRS OF POTS THAT ARE THE SAME DESIGN.

Petroglyphs/Pictographs

Indian carvings are called petroglyphs. Artists pecked or scratched designs onto rocks and cliffs.

The designs are called pictographs if they have been colored with rock or plant material.

Perhaps these symbols of ancient man told stories of trips and adventure. Use the symbols shown below to write your own story of today.

USE SYMBOLS TO WRITE YOUR OWN STORY

How the Canyon Was Discovered

The park ranger told Becky and Andy that Spanish soldiers, led by Captain García López de Cárdenas, first saw the Grand Canyon in 1540. The soldiers were searching for the fabled "Seven Cities of Gold" and instead found the Grand Canyon. They were the first non-Indians to discover the canyon.

After three days, Cardenas decided it was impossible to cross the Grand Canyon and left.

More than 200 years later, in 1776, Father Tomás Garcés discovered Havasu Canyon and the Havasupai Indians. He was the first to call the river "Rio Colorado" which means "red river" in Spanish.

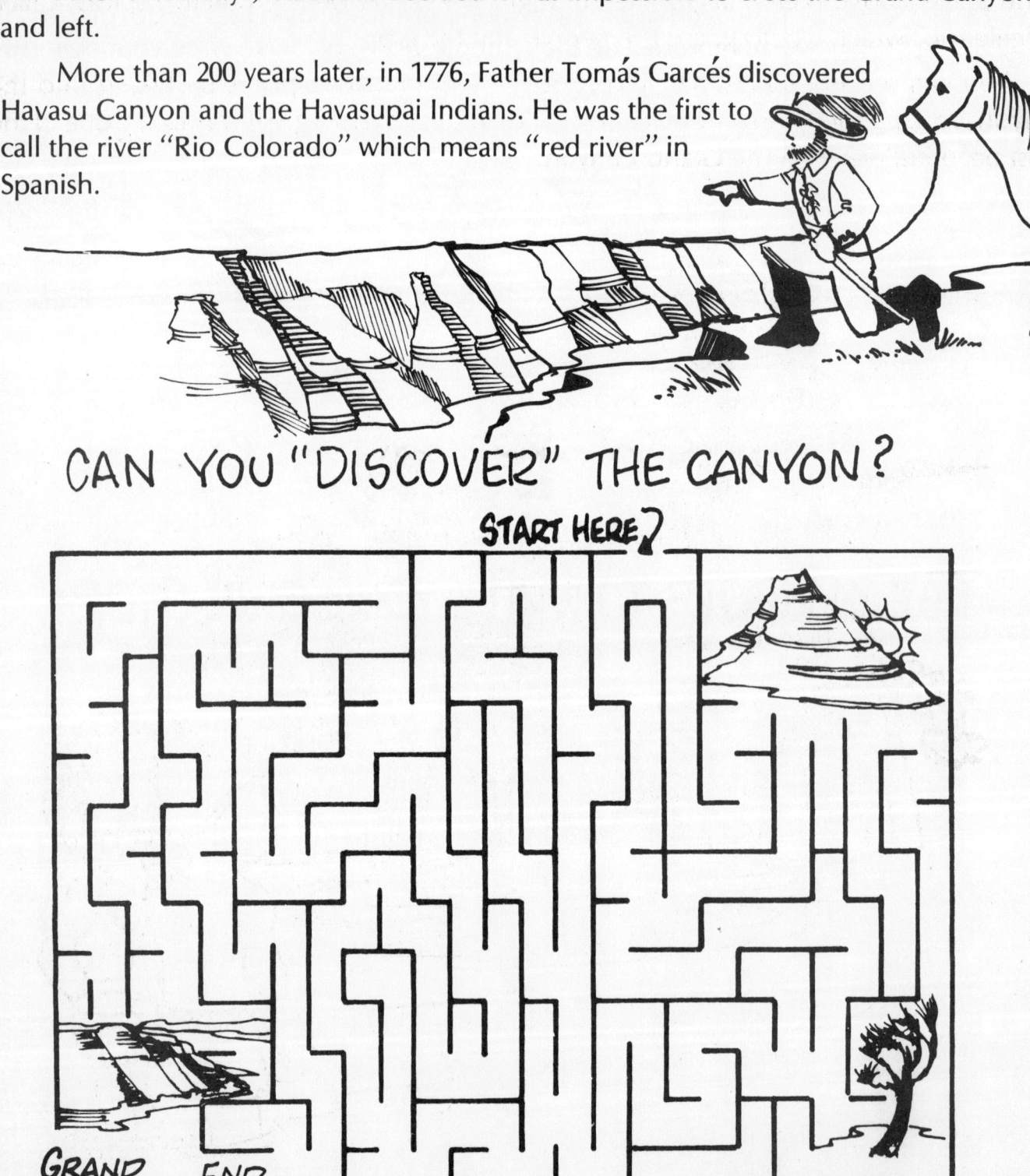

CAN YOU "DISCOVER" THE CANYON?

START HERE

GRAND CANYON END

Havasupai Indians

The Havasupai Indians are the only Indians who live in the Grand Canyon. Their name means "people of the blue-green water." Havasu Creek is nearby and it has a pretty blue-green color. There are four waterfalls along Havasu Creek.

Legend says the Havasupai chose Havasu Canyon as their home because of the two stone pillars above their village. They thought the pillars were protective spirits, called "wigeleeva," which would guard the people and the crops.

You can see the Havasupai village, Supai, and the stone pillars by hiking into the canyon. You must get permission from the Indians first. What a great way to see one of the most beautiful places in the Grand Canyon!

John W. Powell

THE RAFT TRIP OF YESTERDAY

The First Successful River Run

On May 24, 1869, Major John Wesley Powell began his Colorado River journey on the Green River in Wyoming.

On August 13, 1869, he and his crew started down "the Great Unknown." He was entering the Grand Canyon. Powell gave it the name the "Grand Canyon." It had been called "the big canyon."

The Colorado River was so dangerous in some areas, Powell's wooden boats overturned and his supplies were watersoaked or lost.

Then on August 29, 1869, Powell and his men entered safe water. The mighty Colorado River was conquered for the first time! John Wesley Powell was the first "Colorado river runner."

USE THESE WORDS TO COMPLETE THE PUZZLE

HAVASUPAI • ARIZONA • RAFT • GLEN CANYON DAM
WHITEWATER • GRAND CANYON • JOHN W. POWELL • R
NEVADA • COLORADO • EXPLORER • PIONEER • RAPI
GREEN RIVER • EXPEDITION • BOULDERS •

Running the River Today

You can enjoy the exciting adventure of running the river through the Grand Canyon just as Major Powell did! Tour guides lead wild rafting trips through the Grand Canyon.

Large pontoon boats, quite different from Powell's wooden boats, travel through the canyon. Some trips last a week or longer and give you the ride of your life!

THE RAFT TRIP OF TODAY

South Rim

Becky and Andy arrived at Grand Canyon Village. This part of the park is open year 'round and has the most visitors. There are many places to stay. Becky and Andy were very lucky. They had a cabin right on the rim! They could look out their window and see the Grand Canyon!

You can see the Canyon rim by bus, too. The bus stops at several viewpoints along the road. Some of these include Mather's Point, Hermit's Rest and Desert View. At each view point, the Grand Canyon looks different.

When the sun sets, watch the changing colors of the Grand Canyon. How many colors can you see?

North Rim

The North Rim is about 11 airplane miles from the South Rim. To reach the North Rim by car, you must drive more than 200 miles. In the winter, the road is closed. Because it is at a higher elevation, the North Rim receives much more snow.

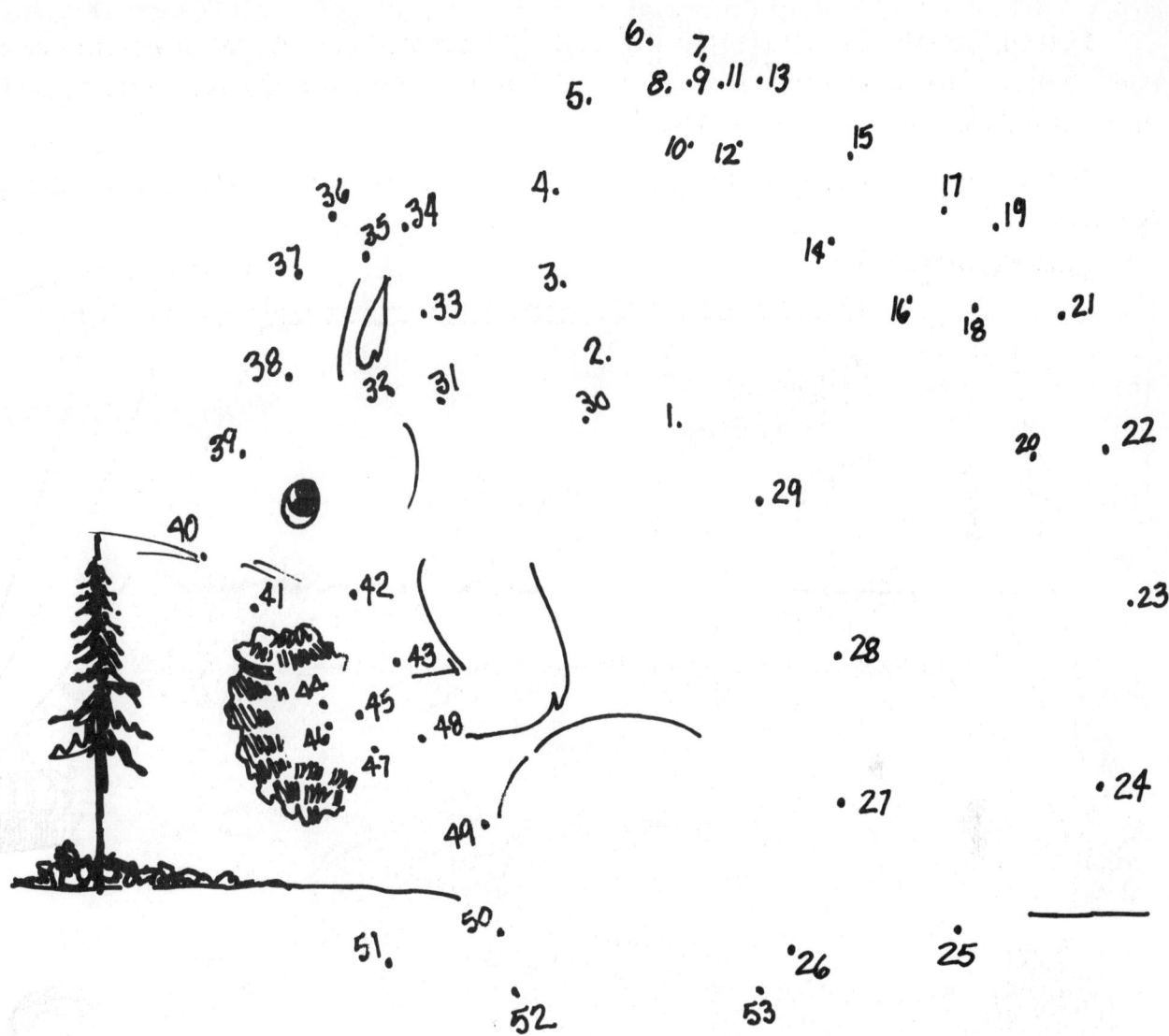

The rare Kaibab squirrel is found only on the North Rim. It has a bushy, all white tail and gray fur, unlike other squirrels. It eats ponderosa-pine seeds and the inner bark of trees.

If you are visiting the North Rim, look carefully. You may be lucky enough to spot the Kaibab squirrel!

Special laws protect these squirrels, which are endangered.

Hiking the Canyon

Hiking into the depths of the Grand Canyon is very popular. It is a great way to see the rock formations and enjoy a "walk through time".

Becky and Andy were very excited about hiking to the bottom of the Grand Canyon. They were prepared! The park service ranger explained the supplies that were needed and made sure the kids had lots of water before he issued them a permit. (One to two quarts of water per person in cooler weather, a gallon per person in hot weather!)

Rules for hiking.

1. Stay on the trail.
2. Do not throw rocks or other objects into the canyon.
3. Do not collect plants, animals, or artifacts without a permit.
4. Do not build open fires.
5. Do not swim in the Colorado River.

The ranger reminded the kids it would take about twice as long to hike back up as it did to hike down. They made arrangements to camp at Phantom Ranch, at the bottom, overnight.

The kids made a list of the hiking rules. Can you see why each one is important?

Write your rules here.

My Rules

Bright Angel and Kaibab Trails

There are several trails into the Grand Canyon. They were first made by deer, bighorn sheep, Indians and prospectors.

The two major trails maintained by the Park Service are the Bright Angel Trail and the Kaibab Trail. The Kaibab Trail is the only one that reaches from rim to rim.

The kids hiked the Bright Angel Trail. When they saw a mule party, they knew to stand quietly along the side of the trail until the mules passed by.

As you hike, it is fun to sing a song. See the song that Becky and Andy wrote. Write your song below!

(Sing to the tune of "A Farmer In The Dell")

A hiking we will go,
A hiking we will go,
In rain and sun and sleet or snow,
A hiking we will go.

We'll hike until we drop,
We'll never, never stop,
In rain and sun and sleet or snow,
We'll hike until we drop.

Indian Gardens

Becky and Andy started down the Bright Angel trail. As they dropped farther and farther into the canyon, they were surrounded by colorful rocks, cliffs and buttes. Up ahead they could see a grove of trees called Indian Gardens.

They arrived at Indian Gardens in time for lunch. As they ate under the shade of the trees, they watched the frogs, lizards, butterflies, and birds. There were even minnows in the creek.

The Havasupai Indians lived and farmed along the creek until the Grand Canyon Park was established in 1919.

Which animals do you see? _____

Phantom Ranch and the Trail UP!

Phantom Ranch is an oasis for all the brave souls that have hiked down from either rim. There are cabins, a lodge, food and showers.

A real bed never felt so good to Becky and Andy as it did after their hike!

The next day they were ready to begin their journey up, up, up to the top.

What would you take with you on your hike?

Mule Rides

Mule rides are a fun, exciting way to reach the bottom of the Grand Canyon. Mules are also used as pack animals to carry in supplies.

It is exciting and scary to be on the mule and look over the edge of the narrow path. You may think the animal is about to walk off the edge because his head is facing one way and you are facing the other! But, mules are known for their sturdy, sure-footed abilities, so you will have a safe, fun time!

Mules are easily "spooked." When mules pass hikers on the trail, the hikers must step quietly to the side of the path until all mules have passed.

Can you see why it is very important for hikers to stand quietly?

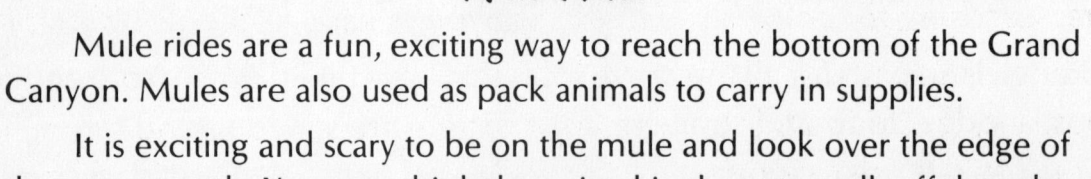

DRAW YOUR OWN PACK MULE HERE AND NAME IT!

NAME

Prospecting in the Canyon

Prospectors, searching for gold, came to the Canyon as early as the 1870's to try their luck.

They built trails and cableways into the canyon. There are still tools and old mines to discover as you explore the canyon.

Other people became greatly interested in seeing this wonder when they heard the miners' colorful stories. Tourism flourished and the miners discovered tourism was more profitable than mining. Soon mining stopped.

Find the hidden bag of gold!

Life Zones

When you journey to the bottom of the Grand Canyon, you experience changes in the environment. The plants and animals are different. The climate is different. It is like traveling from Canada to Mexico. These changes are all due to the altitude. They are called "life zones." The Grand Canyon has four "life zones:" Lower Sonoran, Upper Sonoran, Transition and Canadian. The elevation ranges from 1,200 feet at the river to 7,900 feet at the North Rim. Can you guess where the desert is found and where the alpine forest is found?

1. PONDEROSA PINE 2. KAIBAB SQUIRREL 3. NORTHERN PLATEAU LIZARD 4. MULE DEER

Biotic Communities—the Plants and Animals

Each life zone has its own special plants and animals. Although these plants and animals may live elsewhere, they are much more abundant in their own "biotic" community.

There are six biotic communities in the Canyon. They are called pinon-juniper woodland, desert scrub, yellow-pine woodland, spruce-fir forest, mountain grassland, and streamside.

ZONE 2

5. UTAH JUNIPER 6. RAVEN 7. BANANA YUCCA 8. CLIFF CHIPMUNK
9. DESERT COTTONTAIL

ZONE 3

10. GRAY-HEADED JUNCO 11. BLUE SPRUCE 12. ASPEN 13. GROUND SQUIRREL
14. KENTUCKY BLUEGRASS   15. MULE DEER

ZONE 4

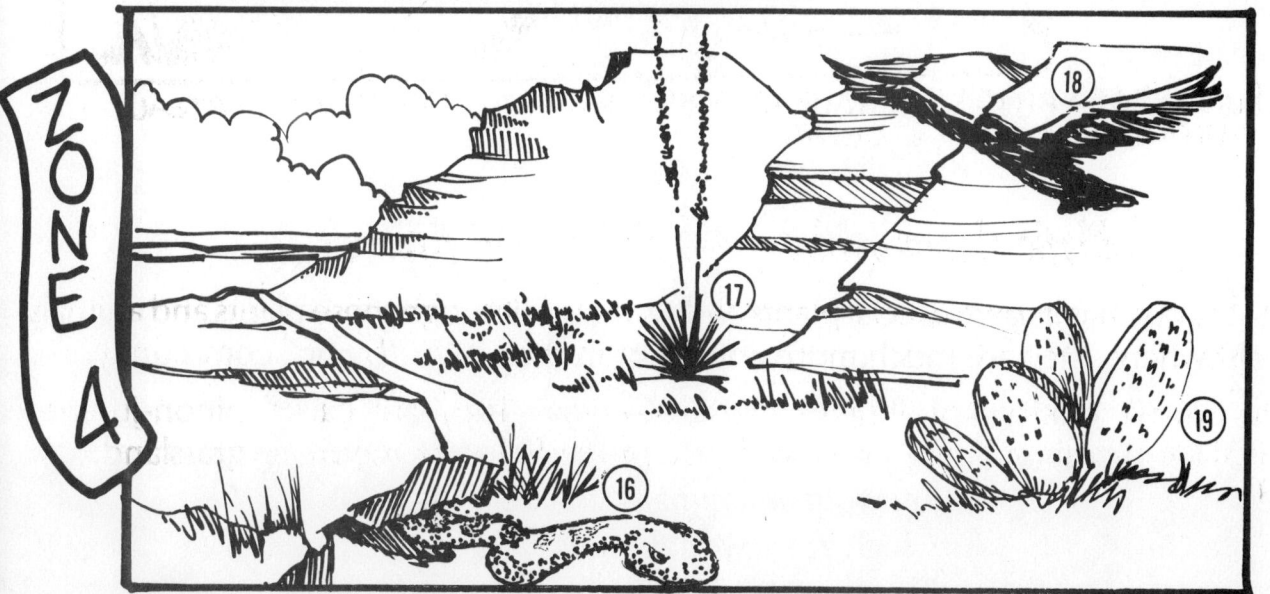

16. GRAND CANYON RATTLESNAKE 17. UTAH AGAVE 18. TURKEY VULTURE
19. BEAVERTAIL CACTUS

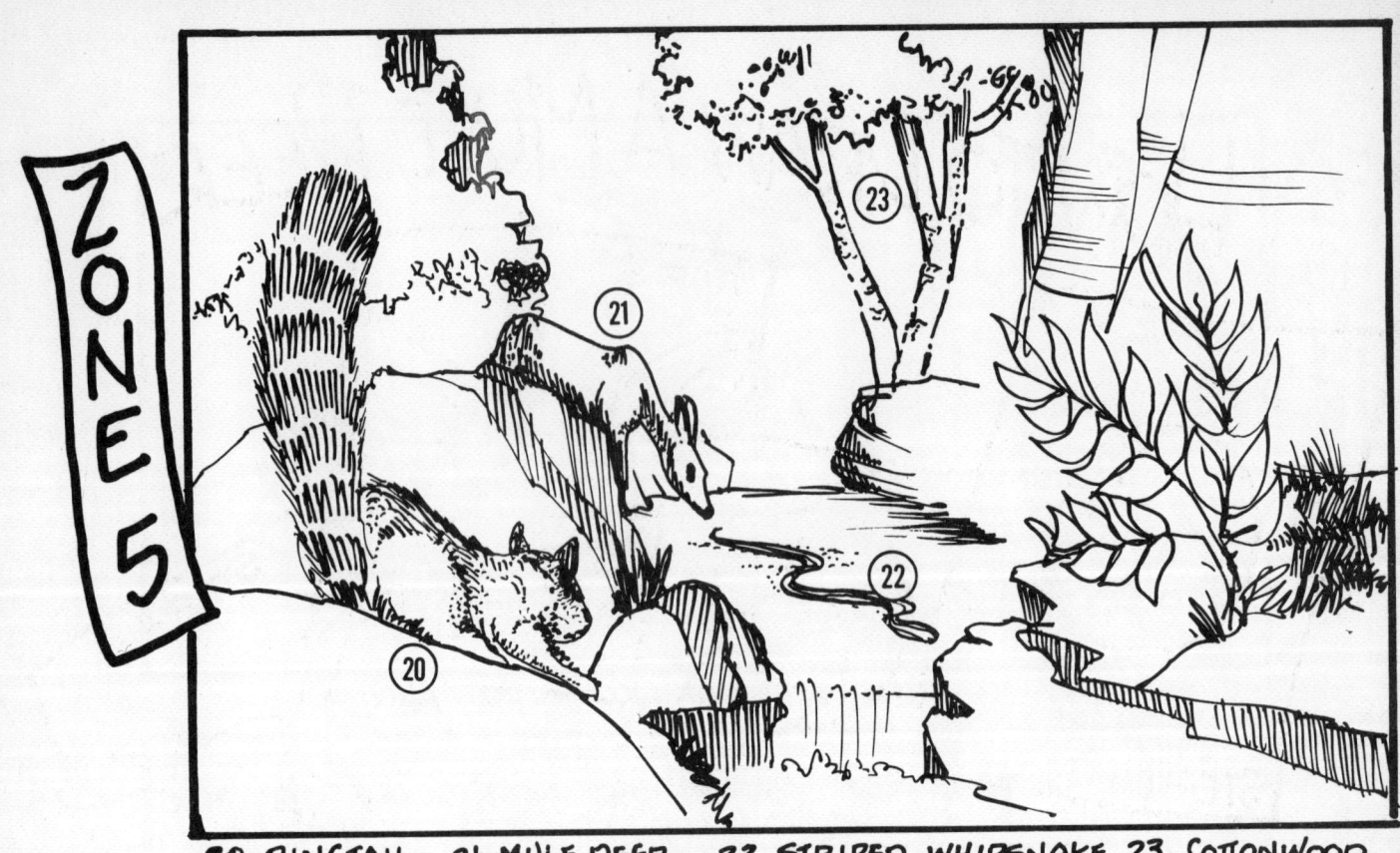

20. RINGTAIL   21. MULE DEER   22. STRIPED WHIPSNAKE   23. COTTONWOOD

Test Yourself

1) In what zone can you find the Grand Canyon rattlesnake? _____

2) In what zone can you find the aspen trees? _____

3) In what zone can you find the Kaibab squirrel? _____

4) In what zone can you find the cottonwood tree? _____

5) Name the animal that you can find in more than one zone. _____

6) If you were an animal, which zone would you choose to live in? _____

There are lots of activities to do when you visit the Grand Canyon! You can see a movie at the IMAX theatre, join a Park Ranger for a nature walk, ride the train from Williams, fly over the canyon in a helicopter or plane and shop for great souvenirs!

Becky and Andy discovered what a special place the Grand Canyon is. They learned that all the living plants and animals depend upon each other for survival.

To keep this delicate balance, no one should feed the animals or disturb the natural environment.

We should keep the Grand Canyon just as it is, so everyone can enjoy it.

Answer Page

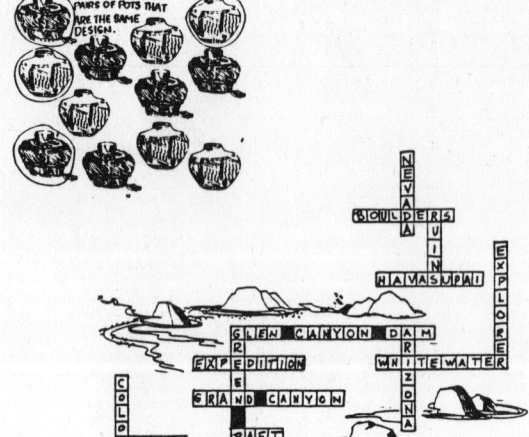

Test Yourself

1) In what zone can you find the Grand Canyon rattlesnake? __4__
2) In what zone can you find the aspen trees? __3__
3) In what zone can you find the Kaibab squirrel? __2__
4) In what zone can you find the cottonwood tree? __5__
5) Name the animal that you can find in more than one zone. __MULE DEER__
6) If you were an animal, which zone would you choose to live in? _____

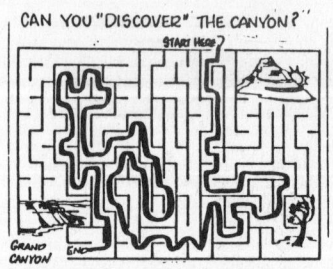

Other Books by American Educational Press

Desert Discovery!
Follow Becky and Andy as they discover the plants and animals of the desert. Puzzles, word games, desert safety tips and mazes add to the fun!

(Grades 1 through 6)

Arizona is for Kids!

Join Becky and Andy as they tour the Grand Canyon State. Visit Lake Powell, Old Tucson, Sedona and more! Discover with them the wonders of Arizona.

(Grades 1 through 6)

New Mexico is for Kids!
From colorful hot air balloons near Albuquerque to ancient Indian pueblos, New Mexico is an exciting adventure. Join Becky and Andy as they experience Santa Fe, Taos, the Rio Grande and much more!

(Grades 1 through 6)

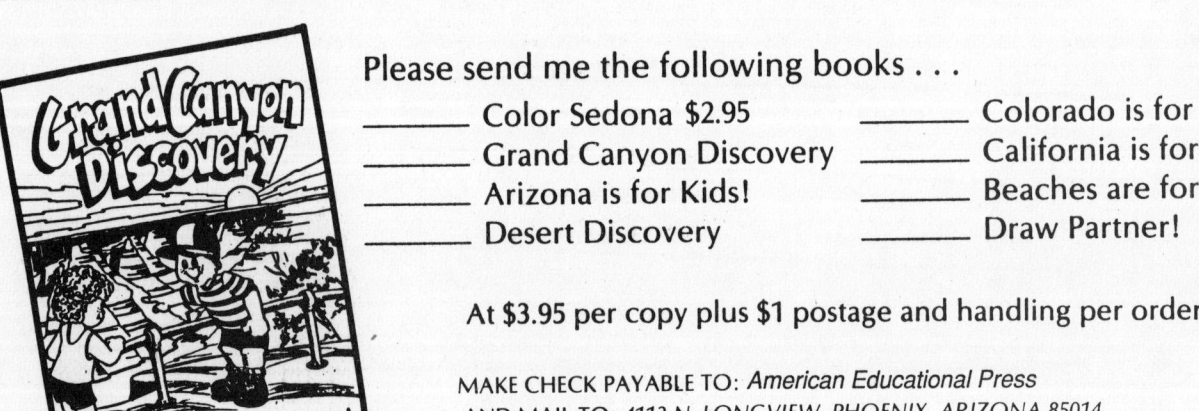

Please send me the following books . . .
- _____ Color Sedona $2.95
- _____ Grand Canyon Discovery
- _____ Arizona is for Kids!
- _____ Desert Discovery
- _____ Colorado is for Kids!
- _____ California is for Kids!
- _____ Beaches are for Kids!
- _____ Draw Partner!

At $3.95 per copy plus $1 postage and handling per order.

MAKE CHECK PAYABLE TO: *American Educational Press*
AND MAIL TO: 4113 N. LONGVIEW, PHOENIX, ARIZONA 85014

Name _____
Address _____
City _____ State _____ Zip _____